Old Shandong

威廉·史密斯的第二故乡

Reverend William A.Smith's Shandong

Gerald B.Sperling （施吉利）
宋 家 珩 （**Song Jiaheng**） 编

山东美术出版社
Shandong Fine Arts Publishing House

老山东

策划： 李　新

设计： 周　正

编辑： 孙顺正

　　　　周　申

英文

审校： 黄毓麟

鲁新登字 04 号

出版： 山东美术出版社

　　　（济南经九路胜利大街 39 号）

发行： 山东美术出版社出版发行

印刷： 北京百花彩印有限公司

　　　787×1092 毫米　12 开本

　　　9 印张 4 插页 20 千字

　　　1996 年 12 月第 1 版　1996 年 12 月第 1 次印刷

　　　印数：1-3,000

ISBN 7-5330-0993-2/J·992

定价：68.00 元

出版者的话

孔子曰："德不孤，必有邻。"

一位加拿大老人到了垂暮之年仍旧对中国有着深深的眷恋，88岁的人还念念不忘打起行李再来山东。这种超越国界的友谊和情感，也打动了大洋彼岸我们的心。

作为出版者，我们面对着这些本世纪初的历史照片，就好像面对着60年前的中国。60年前的那个时代是一个旧的时代，也是中国人民沉重的岁月。用我们手中的笔叙述过去是必要的，而威廉·史密斯先生的照相机记录的画面，为我们保存了一份难能可贵的历史佐证。

在我们把本书定名为《老山东》时，我们发现威廉·史密斯先生60年前不仅用他的眼睛注意到了当时山东的方方面面，而且他的摄影技术也有独特的艺术风格，完全可以同专业人员相媲美。

今天，在该书得以出版之际，我们希望这本书能使更多的人全面了解和认识中国的过去，也让我们为中国更好的未来而祝福！

感谢作者、编者和加拿大驻华大使馆为本书出版做出的努力和贡献。

山东美术出版社
1996.4.6

A WORD FROM THE PUBLISHER

Confucius, the ancient Chinese ideologist, once stated, "A virtuous man never stands alone; he will always have friends."

A 90 year old Canadian has for decades cherished memories of China. His boundless friendship and deep feelings for our country are inspirational to us on this side of the Pacific.

As publishers, looking at these photos, we have been transported back to the China of the 1930s. During thar period, life was miserable, full of hardship. Reverend William Smith's photos are testimonials to China's history.

In publishing "Old Shandong", we recognize that Reverend William Smith's sharp eyes captured many aspects of old China. Furtheunore, his distinctive photographic style and artistic vision are timeless.

Today, as we are publish "Old Shandong." we hope that it will enhance understanding of China's past. With such understanding, China's future will be blessed.

Finally, we want to thank Reverend William Smith, Professors Gerald Sperling and Song Jiaheng and the staff of the Canadian Embassy in China for all of their efforts to ensure the publication of "Old Shandong."

Shandong Fine Arts Publishing House
October 1996

前　言

　　威廉·史密斯是加拿大传教士，奉教会派遣于 1931 年 2 月前来中国，先后在湖南、山东、四川等省传教。他是一位摄影爱好者，在中国期间，他在各地拍照，特别是 1934－1937 年间在山东阳谷、莘县、寿张、东阿、聊城等地拍摄了数千张照片，广涉城乡面貌、农业劳作、集市商贸、社会生活、风俗人情、宗教活动等各个方面，大部分均为上乘之作，极具艺术感染力。照片本身就是历史，它们再现了 30 年代的中国社会，特别是山东鲁西地区的风貌，是当今极难寻觅到的珍贵历史资料。我们从中挑选了一百多幅精品，以飨读者。

　　《老山东》一书得以在中国出版是中加学者共同努力的结果，也是中加人民友谊的结晶。

　　加拿大里贾纳大学政治系施吉利教授是一位热心推动加中文化交流的学者，曾多次访问中国。1988 年春，他在里贾纳市寓所接待了一位远方客人杰里米·艾德尔曼。杰里米的母亲玛格丽特·多萝西是威廉·史密斯的长女，1936 年在中国出生，她也是施吉利的挚友。正是通过杰里米，施吉利得以了解其外祖父丰富的摄影珍藏，也是在他的陪同下，施吉利对威廉·史密斯进行了首次采访。所以，我们首先要感谢杰里米·艾德尔曼博士，他应是出版本书的首倡者。

　　山东大学历史系宋家珩教授长期从事加拿大研究，是一位热心推动中加文化交流的学者，多次前往加拿大进行学术访问。1991 年，我们在里贾纳大学一起探讨了本书在中国出版的可能性，并决定为付诸实现而努力。后来，在我们的朋友孙英葵女士的引荐下，找到了出版者——山东美术出版社。

　　本书在编辑出版过程中，得到了加拿大驻华大使馆文化处的经费资助，文化参赞王仁强博士自始至终给予了关怀和支持。

　　此外，艺术摄影师洛恩·麦克林顿高度评价史密斯的作品并给予了许多帮助。里贾纳大学校长基金和文学院两位院长提供了项目的启动费用。施吉利的妻子和合作者玛吉·西金斯从各方面予以关怀和推动，并分享成书的喜悦。李天安教授帮助查阅了有关30年代山东政治、经济、民情风俗的背景材料，为诠释照片提供了依据。史密斯的妻子维拉积极支持本书的出版并给予诸多关照。我们向以上所有关心和帮助《老山东》出版的领导、朋友和亲人表示诚挚的谢意。

　　当然，本书得以面世的首功当属威廉·史密斯先生，是他的照相机记下了山东历史的足迹，而历史的主角是山东人民，正是他们的坦诚、正直和友好激发了史密斯的艺术灵感。

　　本书选登的照片绝大多数摄自山东鲁西地区，只有少数几幅拍于湖南、北京、天津。相当一部分的拍摄具体地点和时间已无从查考，我们只能根据史密斯的回忆和可能收集到的资料进行诠注，错误之处在所难免。本书的前言，照片诠释和介绍史密斯先生的文章虽采用了中英文对照的形式，但考虑到中外读者的不同需要，内容上不尽相同，特此说明。

施吉利

宋家珩

1996 年 10 月

于山东大学

PREFACE

This book has had a history, not nearly so eventful as Reverend William A. Smith's story, but interesting all the same. After spending some three years in China, from 1985-1987, Gerry Sperling returned to Canada to take up his teaching position at the University of Regina. Sometime in the spring of 1988, he received a call out of the blue from a decades old buddy, Howard Adelman. He informed him that his son, Jeremy, then in his late twenties, was doing research on his Ph.D. dissertation comparing economic developments on the Canadian prairies and Argentina from 1900-1914. He had to spend some time in the Saskatchewan Archives in Regina. Could Sperling find this young man a place to stay? Certainly he could, and did.

He had not seen Jeremy since he was a tot and they soon were engaged in a wide range of discourse. Sperling was regaling this young historian with some of his tales of China, when Jeremy interrupted and said,"You know grandpa has this incredible collection of photos he took when he was a missionary in China."

It took Sperling a moment to place"grandpa" . And then it all came back. As it happened, some thirty years previously, Jeremy Adelman's mother and Sperling had been friends. He remembered her telling him that she had been born in China and that her dad was a missionary. In fact, she is the Margaret Dorothy Smith who was born in Hebei province on September 19, 1936.

One thing led to another and on several occasions, first with Jeremy and then alone, Sperling embarked on a series of lengthy interviews and photos viewing with Will Smith in Clrksburg, Ontario, Canada. Dr. Jeremy Adelman, then, is the first person who should be thanked. He was there at the inception of an idea. Certainly, Jeremy's father and mother should be acknowledged as well. After all, without them there would be no Jeremy. Then again, without Will and Evangeline, there would be no Margaret.

Four years ago, Professor Song Jiaheng of China's Shandong University, in conversation with Professor Sperling in Regina realized that this book *should and could be published in China*. She found the publisher through her acquaintance with Madame Sun Yingkui,whose husband Sun Shunjun worked as an editor at the Shandong Fine Arts Publishing House. As it happened, Ms. Sun had boarded at Professor Sperling's house when she was a visiting scholar at the University of Regina in 1988.

There are other persons and institutions who have helped along the way in bringing this project to fruition. Dr. Richard King, Counsellor (Academic and Cultural Affairs)at the Canadian Embassy in Beijing, in these times of restraint, managed to find just the right amount of funds to assist in this book's publication. More importantly, he provided moral support for the project when it was needed.

Lorne McClinton, formerly of the School of Journalism and Communications at the University of Regina should be thanked. As an artistic photographer, he recognized the value of Will Smith's work.

The University of Regina's President's Fund and two Deans of Arts provided some important seed money at key junctures in the history of this project. Sperling's wife and partner, Maggie Siggins prodded him, cajoled him and cheered him. One could not ask for a more stimulating life mate. Song's husband, Li Tianan, an economic historian, provided many useful insights into the Shandong political economy of the 1930s. Vera Smith, Will Smith's wife, supported Will and was keen about this project from the beginning. Will Smith is a lucky man to have such a wife.

Of course, the hero of the piece is the Reverend William A. Smith. Without his eye, none of this would have happened. But perhaps the real giants are the people of Shandong who were there to inspire Will Smith's art. The vast majority of the photos displayed in this book are from Reverend Smith's Shandong period, 1934-1937. There are a few photographs from Beijing, Hunan and Tianjin. Smith kept fairly precise records for most of his photos. On the other hand, many of his photos are identified generally by place and time. We have for the most part relied on his memory.

While we have tried to present the description of Will's life and work from his perspective, in the final analysis, we are responsible for the interpretation presented in this book.

Gerald B. Sperling   Song Jiaheng
Jinan
October 1996

搭车赶集
An oxcart, laden with happy people:"On the road again."

1

轿车
A major form of transportation of people or goods

集市

The market was very important in the life of the people of Shandong. There were markets every three days, every week and in some places there would a semi-annual or annual fair.

集市一角

Masses of people at a market within the city walls.

帽子摊
The hat market to satisfy the tastes of every size and fashion desire.

鞋 摊
Shoes for sale. Note the "bound feet", top centre.

5

卖铁器货摊

Metal utensils for sale. It must be just after lunch because one of these entrepreneurs is having a *xiuxi* or rest.

在集市上卖京花
Jing Hua. These imitation flowers were used to decorate women's hair.

待售的新娘嫁妆
Wedding chests.

酒、油零售车
Wine, Cooking
oil, key staples.

斗、升

Some staples, beans,
corn, flour. But note
the measuring devices,
going from the smallest,
sheng, to one *dou,* to two
dou. These measures are
no longer in use.

卖旧货、杂货地摊
Recycling used
dongxi, "stuff".

皮货商
The fur man
from Hebei.

卖土布的妇女

These cottage clothmakers are waiting to sell the cloth that they have spun and woven themselves.

卖馅饼

People have to eat at the market and here are making meat or vegetable pies, *xian bing*.

卖馓子和挂面

Dried noodles, *gua mian*, on the right and the traditional *sanzi*, or fried flour in the shape of noodles, but they're not noodles.

文具书摊
Pens, ink, inkstones, brushes, paper and books: a haven for intellectuals in the market.

集市卖画
Local artists also put their work up for sale along the city walls.

旧货摊
Used clothes, cotton for recycling.

小百货店和裁缝

Taitor and general store where customers could purchase everything from tea kettles to dry goods.

拉洋片

"Moving" pictures in a Shandong market. It's not clear why the smiling man has hung a skin on a pole. Perhaps, it is to attract a crowd.

卖馍的小贩
Steamed bread on a stick. This method of display cannot be seen in the 1990s.

生意兴隆

Business is brisk. Cloth and silk from the big city, Beijing, at least that's what the sign indicates.

逛集市

Sometimes an elaborate market would be organized outside the city walls.

阳谷街头换钱人

Money changer. Such persons played an important role in China in the 1930s. During the warlord period of the 1920s, a myriad of currencies came into circulation.

阳谷集市上换钱者

Coinchanger.

卖带子的老人

Will Smith called this photo, "The Peddler of the Garter." In fact, he was selling a kind of belt designed to keep one's pants from falling down. He was "A Sash Peddler" in Yanggu, Shenxian, Echeng.

赶　集
To the fair!

寿张县城门楼

Gate in the Shouzhang city wall.

东昌（今聊城）街景，远处是光岳楼
Guangyue Lou(Sunshine Mountain Temple)at the
end of a street in Dongchang (now Liaocheng).

东昌（今聊城）牌坊
Dongchang(now Liaocheng)Paifang(a
memorial arch made of stone).

运棉骡马大车受阻（东昌牌坊局部）
Detail of carving on Dongchang Paifang.

阳谷街道前廊
Another Yanggu
street scene.

阳谷县修自行车店铺
"Hanging out" on Yanggu street.

阳谷县城内街景
Street in Yanggu.

黄包车
Rickshaw.

寿张具城墙拐角
Shouzhang city wall.

维修城墙
Repairing the Yanggu wall, December 1936.

城门洞
City gate. Note the cigarette ad. on the left.

古槐、店铺
City scene. Note the preservation and use of an ancient tree.

黄牛大车
To market.

小杂货铺
Confectionary, Shandong,
1930s.

绸布店
Fabrics shop, silk,
wool, cloth.

莘县宝塔
Shenxian Pagoda.

迎 亲

Normally, the bride would be conveyed to her husband-to-be in such a chair, Yanggu.

新娘下轿

The bride being led to her fate, that is, the groom, Yanggu.

婚 礼
Child bride and groom, Yanggu.

喜 丧（天津）
A wealthy older person's funeral procession, Tianjin.

34

路 祭

This paper image of the dead man will be burned at the graveside to ensure that he will go to heaven, Shandong.

出殡队伍在行进中

The male friends and relatives of the deceased are leading the coffin towards the graveside. They in turn are being led by the hired funeral band, Shandong.

守 灵
Mourning the deceased, Shandong.

哭 丧
Normally, the mourning women friends and relatives would follow the coffin, Shandong.

37

灵　柩

The coffin.

出大殡（天津）

A wealthy person's funeral procession. Rear view, Tianjin.

家有丧事

When a person died in North China, it was traditional to decorate the front of his (her) dwelling with paper lions and with Chinese characters depicting the greatness of the deceased. Shandong.

出大殡（天津）

A wealthy person's funeral procession. Front view, Tianjin.

搭台唱戏

Travelling troupes of opera players would tour the countryside giving performances in county seats, towns and villages. This is a summer performance. Note the straw hats. Shandong.

看大戏
A winter performance.

大戏台

A Chinese opera performance in the county seat, probably Yanggu.

卖艺为生的盲人
Smith captioned this picture, "Three blind beggar musicians on the highway."

铁路旁的垃圾堆

The town dump. Children and dogs fight over scraps.

集市艺人
A performer in the
market, Shandong.

少年习武

In North China, *Wu Shu*, or martial arts is imbedded deep in the culture, so that it would not be unusual to see the very young practising. Shandong.

马戏"演员"

Circus Bear in Yanggu, 1936. It seems to be taking a walk.

赶 路
Taking a donkey trip, Shandong.

晚 饭
Traditional Shandong food. A still life of rice gruel, pickled vegetables, millet. Will Smith called this a "missionary's dinner."

龙骨水车
The ancient art of
Chinese irrigation.

冬 忙
Masses of peoplè
constructing a canal or
a large irrigation ditch
along the Yanggu wall.

阳谷县城内拾粪、捡柴人
Gathering "night soil" in front of the Smith's wall, Yanggu.

刨大树
Getting to the "root" of the problem.

收工归来
The end of a long
day's labours.

制 瓮
Make the vats.

运土坯
Pushing and pulling a Chinese wheel barrow full of bricks.

晒　纸
Drying the paper on the wall.

运大瓮
Taking the vats to market by wheel barrow.

用四轮车运秫秸
Red Sorghum harvest. At harvest time, sorghum is indeed red in colour.

土窑烧砖
The brick kiln.

盖房上梁
A new house is
emerging in
Shandong.

编筐人和独轮车
Basketmaking and wheel
barrow in Yanggu.

锯 木
Sawing lumber.

收小花生
Sieving the peanuts
from the soil.

晒粉皮
Drying *fenpi*, a north
China specialty made
from peas.

老 农
Time is written on the face of this tough old man.

络纱的妇女
Spinning. Note the bound feet.

父与子
Father and Child.

晚　年
The beauty of old age.

一伙年青人
Young peasants posing.

富家女人
Young woman in the afternoon sun.

沿街乞讨
Beggar.

乞讨的残疾人
Beggar.

无家可归
Beggar in the market.

乞 讨
Beggars.

农民和孩子
Peasant and children.

采购归来
Coming home with supper, pork and Chinese cabbage.

中年妇女

Five women, a boy(Paul?) and a dog.

太重了（湖南）
The burden of youth, Hunan, 1933.

小媳妇

Mrs. Chen. Reverend Smith
tells the story of how this
woman was at one time
"possessed by the devil."
Shenxian, 1936 1937.

老妇人
The old woman in winter.

绵羊和牧羊人
Boy with sheep.

船民（湖南）
Boat people, Hunan.

一片汪洋
Water, water everywhere.

撑船救人
Boating in the lane.

洪水无情
Flood.

门板当船
A makeshift raft made from what appears to be a door.

城门进水，街上行船
Gate over troubled waters.

城门口行船
Boats at the gate.

水没街道
Streets turned into rivers.

瓮在街河行
Vessels out of vessels.

以瓮代舟
Creativity. Making
a boat out of vats.

灾 民
Refugees from
the flood.

水漫教堂
The flood reaches the church wall.

渡 船
Ferrying the masses during the 1937 Yellow River flood.

灾民临时的家－窝棚
Temporary refugee house.

土坉城门
Sandbags at the gate.

房倒屋塌
Flood damage.

木筏救人
Devastation.

抢　险
The wall and the water.

摄影师：威廉·史密斯

施吉利　　宋家珩

"我在各地拍照"
"我总觉得自己是山东人"

威廉·史密斯热爱中国，热爱中国的人民、土地和山川。这位在世界各地"传播福音"近60年的传教士同时也是一位摄影爱好者，一位充满勇气和好奇心的冒险家。

1907年，他诞生于苏格兰佩斯利城一个小康之家。父亲1917年在第一次世界大战中阵亡。母亲杰西是一位富于探险精神的女性，1925年移居加拿大安大略省，后又与一位英裔加拿大农民结婚。

威廉曾是典型的移民工人。他学过铁匠，在床垫厂当过雇员，干过机床工和制模工。1926年的圣诞节，他是在多伦多两个教堂度过的，宗教改变了他单调的生活，这个瘦高漂亮的年青人决定"伸出我的手……让上帝主宰我的生命"。1927年，他进入渥太华神学院学习神学。

威廉倾心冒险生涯，厌倦平淡乏味的生活。1927年，在聆听了两位传教士介绍中国经历之后，他对中国产生了兴趣，"我越读有关中国的书，就越迷恋中国，我强烈地意识到，上帝在召唤我到中国去。"①1930年，23岁的史密斯在"上帝的意志"和冒险精神的鼓舞下决心东渡。当时他正热恋一位年青的教师伊万杰琳，希望心爱的姑娘能与他同行，但第一次求婚遭到了拒绝，为了表示对上帝忠诚，他只身前往。1931年2月28日，威廉搭乘日本皇后号轮船离开温哥华，3月21日抵达上海。谈到对中国的第一印象时，他说："我为受到的优待和看见街上众多的人群而激动。"从一开始，史密斯看到的似乎都是中国最好的景象，或许是出于乐观精神和善良的愿望，或许他从未认真地关注过他所面对的贫穷、暴力和不公正，一种具有感染力、令人愉快的乐观主义色彩注入了他的摄影作品，这些照片既是真实的写照，又是他个人心态的反映。

在上海逗留数日后，威廉乘火车来到北京，并立即投入了紧张的中文研习。他被老北京的魅力所吸引，钟鼓楼、天坛、胡同、颐和园、明陵、长城……这一切都令他着迷。有一张他站在长城上的照片：手提心爱的照相机，凝视北方……

1931年夏末，他奉命到湖南传教。1933年，伊万杰琳终于来华与他成婚。他们先后在常德、安乡等地传教，并且参与了地方赈灾和卫生保健工作。他们注意遵从地方的风俗习惯，努力适应当地的生活，还学会了湖南话。

1934年，史密斯离开湖南到山东担任教职。途中曾绕道在天津停留，12月12日他们的儿子保罗降生了。

1935年1月，史密斯全家来到有1700个自然村，城内约有7000人口的山东阳谷县。县城有城墙，城周约8公里。与大多数在华的西方传教士一样，史密斯一家住在单独的，设备比较齐全的教会大院内。他描述道，院内"有一排长方形的平顶土屋，供教会的佣工居住；另有三排砖平房，由中国牧师及其家属、客人和仆佣居住。中间是一眼很大的敞口水井。北角有一套砖房，是传教士的居所。整个大院围有夯筑的土墙，4英尺厚，10英尺高，墙土是从院内南角挖取的，取过土的大坑在雨季就变成了我们的池塘"。教会大院的隔壁驻扎着"基督将军"冯玉祥的部队，所以他们感到很安全。史密斯认识冯将军，并听说过他信基督教的故事，诸如他定期用一个软水管喷洗他的士兵，以此作为集体洗礼。

史密斯在山东的传教方式与湖南不同。在湖南，他通常与中国牧师一起步行走村串户宣传福音。在山东，他采用"帐篷布道"。许多村子邀请传教士去，并提供安置帐篷的场所。帐篷很大，可容纳几百人听道。史密斯写道："为什么成百的人都来听道？因为这是很新鲜的事。他们从未见过这么大的帐篷，过去也从未有传教士来过，他们对帐篷和我们都感到新奇。"他还经常到邻近的县城，如莘县、东阿、寿张、东昌（今聊城）等地的村镇布道，检查各分站中国牧师的工作。他在阳谷的生活是忙碌的，除了布道，还要处理许多与教徒相关的事情，如为

关进监狱的教徒说情，帮助困难户，应邀参加各种庆典，甚至主持婚礼等等。

在山东，威廉几乎变成了专业摄影师。此时，他已积累了丰富的摄影经验，他在各处拍照，上千张照片将他在山东的经历，他的朋友和教徒，鲁西的城乡面貌、社会生活、风土人情以及普通百姓的情趣都一一留在了记忆里。他喜欢山东的生活。他写道："在山东的日子，我得到了非常宝贵的经验和巨大的欢乐，我与正直、坦诚的山东人结下了友谊。此后，我总觉得自己是山东人。"1936年9月，威廉夫妇第二个孩子玛格丽特·多萝西的降生给全家带来了更多的乐趣。他们一共有5个孩子，两个在中国出生，两个生于印度，一个生于加拿大。

1937年夏，日本发动了大规模的侵华战争，他们在中国平静的生活被打乱了。正与全家在北戴河度假的史密斯决定只身返回阳谷拿取冬衣。当时从北戴河到阳谷的旅程已十分艰难，铁路运输中断，兵荒马乱，又值黄河发大水。当他到达阳谷的教会大院时，看到"全部院墙都倒塌了，院内全是水，羊圈被毁，所幸的是房屋完好无损，屋内尚未进水……"。威廉虽置身于天灾人祸的困境之中，可他的相机仍在不停地转动，这才使本书得以再现当年黄河水灾的惨景。

考虑到日军的入侵和黄河水灾，威廉全家利用休假的机会于年底返回了加拿大。1946年史密斯再度来华，在四川传教。1949年前往印度。后来，他曾在台湾、爪哇和海地从事教务。

1976年，他的妻子伊万杰琳在加拿大金斯顿市逝世。史密斯怀着一颗破碎的心继续他的海外生涯，他曾在台湾、香港教书，并于1978年、1983年、1985年三次来中国访问。时隔30余年之后重访故地是令人激动的。他漫步于北京的紫禁城；赴河北邯郸市探望昔日阳谷的旧友；不辞辛劳前往山东聊城与教友相聚，共唱圣歌。深深的怀旧情感，使他更为珍爱往日的相片，正是这一本本塞满了黑白照片的相册凝固了永久的记忆。

　　威廉·史密斯是19世纪末至1949年在华的成千名加拿大传教士之一，是他的相机使他与众不同。数千张黑白照片留下了30年代中国社会的真实面貌，记下了山东历史的足迹，也留住了他对这片土地的缕缕深情。

　　1979年3月，他与一位退休的教师维拉·坎普林结婚。现在，史密斯与维拉在加拿大安大略省欧文桑德过着平静的退休生活。然而，冒险的激情仍不时地撞击着时而清醒、时而恍惚的88岁老人的心。1995年11月9日，维拉在接受电话采访时告诉作者："威廉捆好了旅行袋，随时准备乘汽车到多伦多，再搭轮船、飞机……，他在等待召唤，作好了一切准备。"

　　逝去的中国岁月啊！他眷恋，永难忘怀……。

中国山东济南市
1995年12月

　　① 本文所引史密斯语出自：史密斯专著《It Holds the Whole World Together》，1988年施吉利教授对史密斯的访谈录和史密斯未发表的1978年、1983年、1985年三次访问中国的回忆录。

REVEREND WILLIAM A. SMITH: PHOTOGRAPHER

Gerald B. Sperling and Song Jiaheng

"I took pictures everywhere."

"Always... I have considered myself to be a man from Shandong. "

Will Smith loves China; he loves the land, the people, the sights, the smells, the rivers, the mountains. This evangelical missionary who has devoted close to sixty years of his life to "spreading the word" is also sub-consciously an artist and, perhaps closer to the surface, an adventurer with boundless courage and curiosity.

Born in Paisley, Scotland in 1907 into an upwardly mobile family of former cloth workers with a remarkable mother who also must have had an eagerness to explore the unknown*, he spent an incredible life ministering to Chinese, Indians, Indonesians, Haitians, Canadians.

His father died along with of thousands of other young men on Flanders Fields in 1917. Undaunted, his mother, Jesse, undertook an exploratory trip to Canada in 1920. Clearly running a dry goods shop in Paisley was not for her. She returned to Toronto in 1925 and married an English-Canadian farmer.

Young Will was a typical immigrant worker of the 1920s. He was for a while an apprentice to a blacksmith, a hand in a mattress factory and a tool and die maker. But the humdrum life of a carefree, handsome youth ended around Christmas 1926 in Toronto when on two successive evenings, the first in the Mission Hall on Yonge Street and second at the Christie Street Tabernacle, Will Smith found God. "My hand shot up... I will let Jesus Christ rule my life!", he remembered. By 1927, he was enrolled in an Ottawa Bible school, Annesley College. During summer he sold bibles in the Ottawa Valley.

Not too many years after he had received what he believed a divine summons to "serve Christ", the phone figuratively rang again. In 1927, in Ontario, he heard of the experiences of two missionaries who had been in China. The seed was planted. Smith has always been a man of adventure. Had he not been missionary, he would have been a soldier of fortune, or a crackerjack salesman or an itinerant scholar. Life at home would always be too tame for him. But there was something else: "The more I read about China, the more infatuated I became, the more I sensed that God was calling me to that field," he recalled in an interview.

In any event, contacts with several missionaries who had been in China led him to the conclusion that he must go to the "Middle Kingdom". And he did meet with some of the more illustrious proselytizers. For example, in Ottawa, he heard Dr. and Mrs. Howard Taylor speak. Howard Taylor was the youngest son of J. Hudson Taylor, founder of the China Inland Mission in 1865, which brought together the many different and competing Protestant sects in China.

And after having made his decision to accept the "call", Smith sought the blessing of the legendary Jonathan Goforth who by that time 1930

* Most of the factual material in this article comes from two sources: William A. Smith. It Holds the Whole World Together. The Seniors & Company, Hong Kong, 1984, and a series of interviews held with Will Smith at his home in Clarksburg. Ontario in October and November 1988 and in a seniors' retirement home in Owen Sound, Ontario in summer 1994. Citations of this material will either refer to Smith and a page number or Smith interview and a date. Additional information is drawn from an unpublished manuscript by Will Smith, chronicling his travels to China in 1978, 1983 and 1985. The literature on Canadian missionaries in China is vast. Specific citations in this article are from Peter Stursberg. The Golden Hope. United Church Publishing, Toronto, 1987 and Monroe Scott, McClure: the China Years, Penguin, 1985.

was blind and living in the Missionary Rest Home in Mimico on the outskirts of Toronto. Goforth did give him his blessing, although fortunately, as far as can be determined, Smith did not adopt some of Goforth's less savoury attitudes.

The Reverend Goforth probably regaled his younger acolyte with his adventures during the Boxer Rebellion. What Goforth undoubtedly did not say was that western missionaries in China were partially responsible for the Boxer uprising of 1899-1900.

> *In attempting to convert the Chinese to Christianity, they attacked age old Chinese customs and*
> *institutions and disturbed the tranquility of the country... The missionaries appeared to be "tactless,*
> *imperious and unwise." Perhaps the worst offenders were fundamentalist preachers such as the*
> *Reverend Jonathan Goforth who could see no good whatsoever in Chinese civilization and culture:*
> *all was heathenism and idolatry. The missionaries were arrogant in their assertion of righteousness*
> *even though they saw themselves as humble servants of God spreading the gospel and when there*
> *was trouble and their lives were threatened, they reminded the Chinese of their treaty rights, as*
> *Goforth did, and were not slow to appeal to the Imperial Powers for protection. (Stursberg, page*
> *57, See also Munroe Scott, pp. 2-3)*

However, Will Smith, fundamentalist, seems never to have felt uncomfortable or fearful in China. "Across the years, I have walked in countless villages, towns and cities in the interior and have sensed neither hostility nor fear."

In any event, by 1930 it was clear that Will Smith, age 23, whether imbued with the spirit of God or adventure or a bit of both was going to China. But there was a complication. He had fallen deeply in love. Evangeline Warren was young teacher in a one room school in the Ottawa Valley. She returned this passion and was quite prepared to marry. "Will you go to China with me?" he asked. "The girl said no."

It is not clear from Will's memoirs nor from extensive interviews with him some 60 years later why she rebuffed this first offer. She certainly loved this exuberant young man. Perhaps it was his single-minded enthusiasm about this oriental leap that put her off, at least temporarily. It may have been that Will was placing Evangeline in second place behind China. His comments seem to lend some credence to this hypothesis. For example, he writes regarding these events of 1930, "Already I had applied to the Mission Board for service in China and I realized that to find a suitable wife-companion left me little time." Strangely, at this point his romance with Evangeline was in full flower. After the rejection he wondered,

> *Which was more important-to follow one's natural instinct to marry a beautiful girl, settle down*
> *and serve the Lord in Canada or forego one's natural desire by choosing a life of service in*
> *China though that meant serving alone?*

In the end, he chose to go China alone. "It would be disobeying God not to go."

Actually, this little drama which stretched from the Ottawa Valley to Hunan not only reveals the character of Will Smith. His decision was in a sense consistent with one wing of Protestant missionary ideology. That attitude postulated that "...to alleviate the wretched conditions of the poor [in Britain or in Canada] was charity and social welfare and, while worthy enough, had little to do with one's religious duty to carry the Christian Message to the world," especially to those" heathens sunk in misery and sin." (Stursberg, page 19)

But by 1933, Evangeline, too, had seen the light and had heard the call near her home in Lake Dore, Ontario, where God seemed to speak to her and the word was "China". Evangeline had none of Goforth's attitudes. Will cites approvingly her letters from China home to her mother in Canada,

What does a new missionary to China do? Study the language, immerse oneself in Chinese thought and ways, think Chinese and be a Chinese as far as your skin color and propriety will permit in your dealing with the people. Their culture and language is sacred and to learn it is the way to their respect. (Smith, page 40)

Will had left Vancouver for China on February 28, 1931 aboard the old Empress of Japan. As usual, everything had made a memorable impression. For example, there was a stopover in Kobe, Japan. Somebody at the local Christian Mission hired a rickshaw in which he could tour and see the sights. During an interview in October, 1988, the very Reverend Will laughed sheepishly as he told the tale of the rickshaw driver dropping him off at an interesting looking edifice. When he went inside, he noticed some rather elegant young women sitting at tables. Suddenly, he realized that he had been conveyed to a brothel. "Well, I got out of there rather quickly, I can tell you."

The Empress of Japan arrived in Shanghai on March 21, 1931. Smith's first impressions of China? "I was thrilled with privilege of being there and seeing the multitudes of people on the streets." From the beginning Smith seemed to see the best in all situations he confronted in China. Not that he had a Pollyanna approach, it was just that he did not seem preoccupied with the poverty, deprivation, violence and injustice that must have confronted him. The contradiction is that his camera eye was brutally honest and while many of his photos are imbued with that same infectious, sunny optimism, there are many that reveal the truth of China in the 1930s.

After a few days in Shanghai, Smith took the train to Beijing. He immediately plunged into Chinese language study. To spread the word of God, the recipients of the Message had to understand what you were talking about. "My mind was really on 'one track,' namely-language study, I had come to China to share the savior's love, and language was the main medium."

He was fascinated with "old" Beijing, the Bell Tower, the Drum Tower, the Temple of Heaven, the *hutongs*, the Summer Palace, the Ming Tombs, the Great Wall. And while he does not talk about why he took photographs, it seems that his camera and his camera eye were ever-present. Someone took a wonderful shot of the young Will on the Great Wall. There he is gazing to the North and of course, he's carrying his trusty camera. "It was all so exciting and breathtaking."

By the end of the summer 1931, Smith was on the way to take up his appointment in Hunan. But even this voyage had its perils. On the way to Hankou, his ship was pursued by pirates. The pirates gave up the chase, but the adventures continued because Smith, like Noah, found himself deluged. He experienced the great 1931 flood of the Yangze River. And once again, he recorded the magnitude of this phenomenon on film.

When he first came to Hunan, Smith and latterly his young wife, Evangeline, lived in the mission compound in Changde. Smith considered Hunan province to be the most anti-foreign place in China. Certainly, he was aware of the revolutionary traditions of the province, specifically that Changsha in Hunan was the birthplace of Mao Zedong. (Smith, page 35.)

As he would have to do throughout his several moves in China, Smith had to adapt his Chinese accent. As he put it, he had to purge himself of the Beijing *hua* replace it with Hunanese. Soon, his facility in this new dialect was such that he could engage in open air preaching on his own.

A few months after he arrived in Changde he was transferred to Anxiang, 100 miles northeast of Changde. Will Smith willingly participated in famine relief and in a campaign of inoculation against typhoid. All of this preaching and relief work involved substantial foot travel from place to place in Hunan. One night along with his Chinese Pastor, Ai Kuang, he got caught in a rainstorm on the road. They knocked on the door of a poor peasant family, who welcomed them in. Here they were mud bespattered, cold and wet. The family first brought them warm water to wash their feet, and "then to cap all, our host pointed to the curtained bed, and over our protests insisted we turn in for the night. Where they slept was left to our guess. I am glad that I belong to the human family."

Still Smith did fall prey to some stereotyping about Chinese people and that may have been because many of those to whom he preached often were more than a little skeptical of his message. As he said in an interview in October 1988,

> *The Chinese more than other people... can deceive you very easily. They can put on a front*
> *or face... that leads you to believe they are genuine...There is such a thing as "rice Christians",*
> *which is a common expression in China — not in Chinese. We only use it amongst ourselves in*
> *English. In Chinese it is jia mao weishan de, a make believe person. [literally, a pretend*
> *hypocrite].*

In fact, the more one listens to Smith, reads his memoirs, or most importantly, looks at his photographs, the more one recognizes the complexity or even the contradictions of his attitudes towards China and the Chinese. During the same interview in 1988, he mused as follows,

> *They're very careful not to offend a stranger, so they would always go along with you. You*
> *would never find yourself in an argument unless you were argumentative yourself. They'd do*
> *anything to save your face. They don't want you to feel ashamed or to feel that they have worsted*
> *you... They want you to feel good. Anything to save a man's face and you learn to do the same*
> *thing.*

And there is no doubt that Smith, though very observant and even respectful of Chinese customs was always at heart a fundamentalist Christian missionary saving the heathens. While he was stationed in Anxiang he used to walk 80 li(about 26 miles or 41 kilometers) to a place called Yellow Earth Inn. He noted the frequency of wayside temples. Indeed, he took to counting them and found that there were exactly 80 of these temples, a coincidence to be sure, but from Will's perspective "...a striking evidence of the idolatrous religiosity of the local people."

China was in great turmoil during the 1930s. The communists under Zhu De and Mao were attempting to mobilize the people for social change and to fight the Japanese, who had annexed Manchuria in 1931, creating the puppet state of Manchukuo. Their incursions into China would continue until the all out invasion in 1937. There were repeated aggressive actions by the Japanese throughout this period and, inevitably, there were repercussions for the missionaries. After one of these Japanese atrocities, students in Changde demonstrated and put up posters denouncing the Japanese. One mission worker, a James Mason who was staying in the compound at that time, came out and tore their the posters off the walls. Needless to say, the students were outraged and stormed the Mission. With some difficulty, they were persuaded to leave.

When asked why Mason would act in such a fashion some 55 years after these events, Reverend Smith opined that he was "a crazy imperialist minded fellah," adding, " I have never felt that way against the Chinese I'm a guest in their country and I have to behave myself."

In 1934, the Smiths left Hunan to take up a posting in Shandong. Will had certainly enjoyed his sojourn in the south and it is not readily evident why he left. He writes that the Hunan climate was bad for Evangeline's health and it is true that she had been quite ill. However, it seems that the Smiths were never close to the Caswells, the senior missionaries in Hunan. In 1988, Will suggested that perhaps, the Caswells hadn't understood young people. "There was a wall between us." It's important to remember that in 1931, Will was all of 24, full of "piss and vinegar", although he would never cotton to that phrase, and when she arrived 18 months later, Evangeline was also a very young woman. In any event, the Smiths left Hunan and made their way north to Shandong, with a slight detour to Tianjin, where their first child, Paul, was born on December 12, 1934.

In Shandong, Will blossomed as a photographer. This may be because he was getting better with experience or it may be because he was truly happy in Shandong.

These were years of invaluable experience, years of great joy and forming of many friendships
with the simple guileless people of Shandong. Always since, I have considered myself to be 'a man
from Shandong' and they say my Chinese accent invariably gives me away.

And so in mid-January 1935, the Smith family now numbering three found themselves in Yanggu, the county seat for 1700 villages. It was a walled city with a population of 7,000. The walls had a circumference of eight miles, allowing for much cultivation within the city. As was the case with most western missionaries in China, the Smith family was physically somewhat isolated from the "masses" or *laobaixing*. They lived in a compound of several acres, with various structures. There was

... a large rectangular flat roofed building which was used for Church services, three rows of one
storey flat roof brick buildings to house [Chinese] pastors and their families, as well as guests
and servants. In the center was a large open mouthed well and at the north end a one storey
flat roofed brick house for the missionary family. Around the entire acreage was a high mud
packed wall, four feet thick at the bottom and ten feet high. The earth for the wall was taken
from a section within the wall at the south end creating a large excavation which gave us our
own pond in the rainy season. (Smith, page 58)

This almost colonial structural arrangement came complete with a gateman for screening and greeting visitors. Since the well was considered public property, however, strangers and other villagers had access to the inside of the Christian compound and so it was decided to construct yet another wall around Smith's home and garden. As he wryly comments, "Here we were trying to tear down walls and yet forced to live behind walls and more walls."

The Smith family always felt secure in Shandong for another reason. Just outside the main walls of the compound was a regiment of Chinese soldiers belonging to the army of the "Christian" General. Feng Yuxiang. Smith was acquainted with the General and knew the tale of his conversion after the Boxer rebellion. It seemed that the General periodically engaged in mass baptism by spraying his troops with a water hose. It was comforting to the missionary family to be awakened every morning 5 a.m. by a regimental rendering of "Onward Christian Soldiers."

Smith's style of work was different in Shandong from his earlier experience in Hunan. In the latter province, Smith tended to go on foot alone or with a Chinese pastor from village to village and even from home to home spreading the "word." In Shandong, Smith utilized what he called "tent evangelism." Villages would "invite" the Mission to come and set up shop in a vacant lot. The tent was large enough to hold several hundred potential converts. Local contacts would be made with "enquirers", i.e., persons who were having an initial look at Christianity and of course, much of the preaching and proselytizing would be done by Shandong people familiar with the regional dialect . Smith himself clearly had a good ear because soon he "delivering the message" in an impeccable Shandong accent.

Why would people come in their hundreds to these events? Because of the novelty of it.
They had never seen a tent that big before. And never before had any team come. The tent was
a novelty and we were a novelty.

In addition, there was a network of Christian outstations in neighbouring towns and villages such as Shenxian, Echeng, Changzhou, and Dongchang(now called Liaocheng). Smith visited all of these places organizing the work of local Chinese pastors.

It was during this period that Will took some marvelous photos of a traditional Chinese wedding. While the guests appear happy, the very young veiled bride seems cowed and almost frightened. This and other wedding ceremonies were presided over by the Reverend Smith. According to the customs of the time, these marriages would be arranged without the consent of the child bride. When asked if he had any problem marrying Christians under these circumstances, Smith replied in typical evangelical fashion:

No. We never interfered in their family matters. This was their custom. This was the way they did
things and we didn't touch these matters.

Actually, while Smith studiously stayed out of the social concerns of the families he was ministering to, he was aware that Evangeline frequently listened to the problems of the women who would pay her social visits. There were separate women's tents.

Life for the Smiths during the Shandong period was eventful and full of challenges. There were many incidents of Smith ministering to his flock, saving Christains from jail, enduring hardship. On September 19, 1936, the second Smith child, Margaret Dorothy, was born. (The Smiths had five children, two born in China, two in India and one in Canada.) But events of history were interceding on this fascinating life in China.

By the summer of 1937, Japan was becoming increasingly rapacious. The Smith family had decided to spend the summer by the sea in Beidaihe. As the summer wore on, Will became convinced that it would be better for all if he made it back without the family to Yanggu to gather their winter belongings. The trip from Beidaihe back to Yanggu was harrowing. Not only were rail lines cut, aircraft flying overhead and troops moving. The Yellow River was in full flood. Upon reaching the mission compound, he was faced with the following:

All the compound walls were flat and every inch of ground was covered or had been covered by
flood water. Buildings were still holding up, although the goat house had collapsed.. Fortunately,
the flood had not come up to the floor of the house.. To my knowledge Church personnel never
lived in that house again.

But throughout for all this turmoil Will continued taking pictures. Vignettes of the Great Yellow River Flood appear in this book.

By now, Smith realized that it was time to take his leave of China, what with the flood and the Japanese invasion. He was due for a furlough, having spent seven years in the field and by Christmas he was back in Canada, not to return to China until 1946.

One gets the impression from Smith that while he took to ministering in Sichuan after the war with his usual gusto and certainly his camera was still always at the ready, nothing compared to his work in Shandong from 1934-1937. After the war, he could not come to terms with Communist Liberation. In 1949, he managed to remove his family from Sichuan to India where he preached first to Chinese expatriates and then to Indians. After that and beyond the purview of this book, Will spent time in Taiwan, where again he could use his Chinese language facility. He also managed sojourns in Java and in Haiti.

In 1976, his beloved Evangeline died of cancer in Kingston, Ontario, Canada. Broken hearted but undaunted Smith continued his peripatetic ways, teaching in Taiwan and Hong Kong and returning for short and then more extensive tours of People's China in 1978, 1983 and 1985 including a return to his favorite Shandong stomping grounds. (Smith, Unpublished memoirs, 1978, 1983, 1985). Curiously, in his writings about these later visits to People's China, he seems more aware of social matters, that is, what people were wearing, what they are eating, the condition of buildings, than he was during the 1930s and 40s.

His return to Beijing in 1978 was poignant. To be able to see the Temple of Heaven and to walk through the Forbidden City after three decades and more made him nostalgic and in his memoir of the 1978 trip, he makes a rare comment about his photos.

This view of this scenery and art, located in the old Tartar City brings back wistful memories of
my stay in Peking, of cycling her dusty roads... I may not have seen all the sights of Peking in

those days [1931], for my quest was language study, but what I saw left imperishable impressions,
many of which I have in my early black and white picture album.

One of his purposes in returning to China was to visit the people and places connected to his earlier ministry. Thus, during his fall 1985 "China Trip" he made his way to Handan in Hebei province to locate the widow of An Fei Li (Philip An), the blind evangelist who had been a pastor with Will in Yanggu in the 30s. An had "wowed" Shandong Christians and *non-Christians* alike with his use of a Braille bible and his rapturous sermons. And on November 6, 1985, some 50 years after first meeting her, he found An's wife, Cao Lan Bo. She was still a Christian actively practicing her faith.

Four days later, on November 10, 1985, burdened with a heavy cold and in the face of bureaucratic obstruction, Will Smith, aged 78, rose from his bed in a Jinan hotel at 5 a.m. and took the bus to Liaocheng, the former Dongchang, and found the Christian community.

As we entered the meeting house all within rose to greet what was possibly the first foreign face
many of them had seen. They sang a familiar hymn... They then asked me to speak. I then spoke
for 10 to 15 minutes relating God's hand in our lives since we left Yanggu 50 years previously
memory the 23rd psalm... After the service, I took pictures of the group outside. (Smith,"China trip
1985," unpublished memoir, page 13)

In March of 1979, he married for second time to a retired Owen Sound school teacher, Vera Camplin, who was living in Clarksburg, Ontario in apple country on Georgian Bay. When he was interviewed in 1988, Will Smith was still active, giving Mandarin lessons to interested parishioners in the local church.

Will Smith was one of thousands of Canadian missionaries who worked in China from the 19th century until Liberation in 1949. He wasn't a McClure, a Willmott nor an Endicott. Like Jonathan Goforth he was a fundamentalist and as such, he seemed to care more about the salvation of people's souls rather than the health of their bodies, although he modestly writes of famine and epidemic relief work he did while in China. What separates Smith from Goforth and these other worthies is that he is an artist. Will Smith just kept on taking pictures that captured the reality, the joys and the sorrows of life. He doesn't talk about photography much. He much prefers to talk about the need to spread the "seed." However, as important to him as has been his teaching of the gospel, his legacy to the rest of us are those wonderful photographs.

As of this writing, Will and Vera are living quietly in a seniors' complex in Owen Sound, Ontario, Canada. And yet the sprit of adventure still burns within Will Smith. According to Vera, "He keeps a bag packed ready to go, to take the bus to Toronto, to catch a ship, a plane, in case the Call should come. He's ready."

Jinan, Shandong
People's Republic of China
October 1996